Dear Baby, Let's Dance!

By Carol Casey

Illustrated by Jason Oransky

Wake up, Baby! The day's begun.
This is no time to snooze.

Let's get you dressed for family fun.
You'll need your dancing shoes!

"Come float with me on tippy-toes
to sway and leap and twirl.

Let Auntie show you all she knows
to give ballet a whirl!"

"Gran and Pop love ballroom dance.
Around the floor we glide.

Our tango fires up romance
to stay a Groom and Bride!"

"Yo! Uncle Paul can spin it all playing music all night long.

You may be small and like to crawl but you'll dig this hip-hop song!"

"C'mon Baby, stomp your feet
and wave your arms around.

"Your sister wants a word with you.
Some dances are too planned.

I'm gonna teach you to **Shake** that tutu and groove to a rock'n roll band!"

"Uncle John doesn't like to groove.

I'd rather watch a game.

Even Moose can strike a pose.
He likes his music loud.

Wiggle with him nose to nose.
It's sure to please the crowd!

"Daddy likes to waltz with you.
You're my Princess at a ball.

Mommy likes to join in too
for our favorite dance of all!"

'Night 'Night, Baby. Go to sleep
and dance all through your dreams.

Jump that moon with a daring leap
and glide down silvery beams.

What's YOUR favorite
dance move!?!

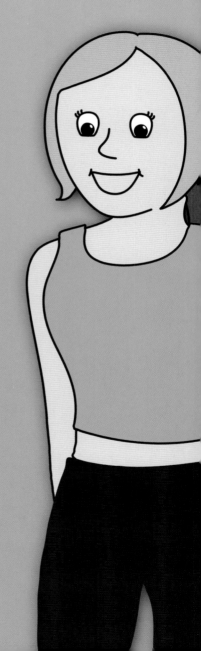

A note from the author:

I love how dancing can link generations in a family. In our house, we all love to turn on the music and teach 2 year old Ava our favorite moves. The very first page I wrote for this book was inspired by a tango that my parents did a few years ago on Christmas Eve. They are 86 and 81 and married for over 60 years so I think it is fair to say that dancing does fire-up romance to stay a groom and bride!

My hope is that you laugh and dance your way through this book and add a few signature moves of your own.

Warmly,

Carol Casey

I invite you to visit

www.dearbabybooks.com

-For information on upcoming books
-Links to fun and educational computer games to play with your
 baby or toddler
-An author blog on family life

For my favorite dance partners

Erin, Leah, Mary, Diana, Pam,Jackie, Sue, Ava,
and to all the VS Dancers

And for Vince and Gloria Bicichi who taught all of their lucky children
how to be a family

ISBN 978-0-9820972-1-2
Publisher Control Number: RPLD0909-1
Distributed by National Book Network 1-800-462-6420
DearBaby Books www.dearbabybooks.com
Printed in Hong Kong

For inquiries to the Publisher,
please email: info@dearbabybooks.com

Other DearBaby Books

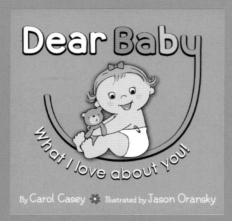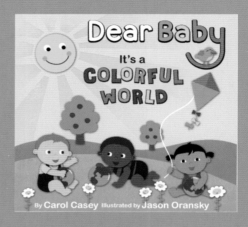

Dear Baby, What I love about you!

A wonderful first book for babies that lets them know why they
are so irresistible. Available in a sturdy board book format.

May 2010

Dear Baby, It's a Colorful World

An endearing cast of multicultural babies, cheerful rhymes,
and vibrant landscapes help young children learn to name and
identify colors, while providing a gentle lesson on diversity.